Meet
Shaquille
O'Neal

Meet
Shaquille O'Neal

by Stephanie St. Pierre

A Bullseye Biography

Random House New York

Photo credits: AP/Wide World Photos, p. 3, 6, 9, 15, 16, 17, 20, 29, 34, 42, 47, 48, 57, 58, 59, 60, 67, 68, 71, 85, 87, 95, 100, 103, 105; Focus on Sports, Inc., p. 14, 19, 37, 51, 54, 61, 93.

A BULLSEYE BOOK PUBLISHED BY RANDOM HOUSE, INC.
Cover design by Fabia Wargin Design and Creative Media Applications, Inc.
Copyright © 1994 by Stephanie St. Pierre
All rights reserved under International and Pan-American Copyright Conventions.
Published in the United States by Random House, Inc., New York, and simultaneously in Canada by Random House of Canada Limited, Toronto.
Library of Congress Cataloging-in-Publication Data
St. Pierre, Stephanie
Meet Shaquille O'Neal / by Stephanie St. Pierre.
p. cm. — (A Bullseye biography)
Summary: A biography of one of basketball's hottest new stars.
ISBN: 0-679-85444-4
1. O'Neal, Shaquille—Juvenile literature. 2. Basketball players—United States—Biography—Juvenile literature. [1. O'Neal, Shaquille. 2. Basketball players.
3. Afro-Americans—Biography.]
I. Title. II. Series.
GV884.054S8   1994   796.323'092—dc20   [B]   93-1678
Manufactured in the United States of America   10 9 8 7 6 5 4 3 2

Contents

Shaquille O'Neal brings the backboard crashing down.

1
A Shaq Attack

It had been an exciting night. It was now the final quarter. The basketball game was almost over. It was March 1993 and the Orlando Magic were playing the New York Knicks in front of a crowd of almost 20,000 cheering fans at Madison Square Garden in New York City.

All night long, the crowd watched as a rookie, Number 32 on the Magic, ruled the court. Then an amazing thing happened: Number 32, the center for the Magic, dunked the ball—and brought the glass backboard crashing down from the rafters, shattering across the floor of the court! The crowd went wild.

Whether or not everyone who saw the game remembers what the final score was that night, or which team won the game, people will certainly remember when Shaquille O'Neal "brought down the house."

In 1992–93, his first season in the NBA (National Basketball Association), Shaquille seemed to receive more attention than any other player in the league. He had signed the highest-paying rookie contract in the history of the NBA—seven years for nearly $40 million! Everyone was waiting and watching to see what Shaq would do next.

By the end of the 1992–93 season, Shaq had pulled down two backboards. And he had scored 1,893 points. But despite having

Shaq with teammate Dennis Scott, after pulling down the backboard at the Meadowlands Arena.

this amazing rookie on the team, the Orlando Magic did not win as many games as they had hoped to. In fact, they did not even make it to the play-offs, winding up the season nearly in last place.

Shaquille had a good year but not a perfect one. The Magic had improved as a team over the course of the season, but they were a young team. They still needed more strong players. All the players needed more time to learn how to work together on the court in order to win. By the following season, they would have new players to help make the team even stronger. They would have many more practices to learn how to work together as a team. Maybe they'd make it to the play-offs in 1994. But until the next season, the Magic were through playing in front of an audience.

Although the Magic were no longer appearing in games on television, Shaq *was* appearing—and often! Thanks to the television commercials he did for Reebok athletic shoes and Pepsi-Cola, no one could possibly forget who Shaq was.

This is the story of how Shaquille O'Neal got the whole world to have a "Shaq Attack."

2

The Center of Attention

At seven feet one inch tall, and weighing a little over three hundred pounds, Shaquille O'Neal—or Shaq, as fans have come to call him—is a giant, even by basketball standards. His hand is nine inches wide and eleven inches long. He can palm a basketball as easily as if it were a grapefruit.

He wears a size 20EEE shoe, which is about twice as big as that of the average man. Shoe size is not measured in inches, though. If you measured Shaq's shoe with a ruler, it would be 15 1/2 inches long, 5 1/2 inches wide, and 9 inches high!

To give you an idea of just how big a size 20EEE shoe is, think about this: A shoelace from one of Shaq's sneakers is five and a half feet long! Here's another way of thinking about it: It would take an entire half-gallon carton of milk to fill one of Shaq's hightops.

Of course, you can't just go into a store and buy size 20EEE shoes. Shaq has to have his shoes made just for him. Custom-made shoes can cost up to $200 a pair. But now that Shaq has his own line of Reebok sneakers he doesn't have to worry about buying sneakers anymore.

Shaquille plays center. It is a position that is often held by especially tall players. Wilt Chamberlain, Hakeem Olajuwon, Kareem Abdul-Jabbar, Patrick Ewing, and David

*Shaq and New York Knicks center Patrick Ewing
wait for a rebound.*

Robinson are, or were, all centers. All of these famous players are also at least seven feet tall.

The average NBA player is between six

and a half and seven feet tall. Of course, being tall makes it easier to get the ball into the basket, which is ten feet from the ground. But there are also some excellent players under six feet tall. For instance, Muggsy Bogues, of the Charlotte Hornets, is only five

Patrick Ewing tries to prevent Shaq from getting a shot.

feet three inches tall (a few inches shorter than Shaq's shoelace!).

Height isn't the only advantage a player can have. Shaquille is not only tall, he is also very heavy. You might think that a 300-

Shaq's size makes it easy for him to block opponents like Miami Heat forward John Salley.

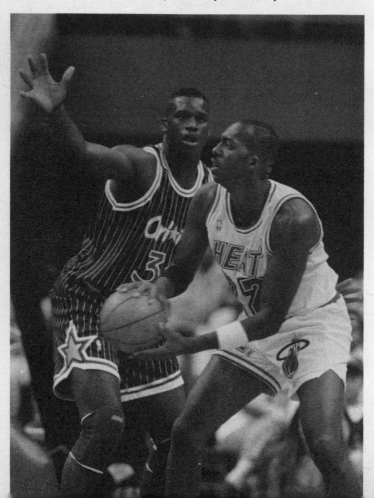

Shaq powers past his opponents.

pound man is fat, but in Shaq's case almost all of his weight is muscle.

That much muscle makes Shaq extremely strong. And amazingly enough, it wasn't

17

until his first year in the NBA that Shaq began exercising with weights to *increase* his strength.

His tremendous size and strength are big factors in the way that he plays basketball. His approach is called a power game, because he puts so much pure physical power into moving the ball around the court.

Many of the really big basketball players are not as fast or as agile as their shorter teammates. But despite his size, Shaq can run and move very quickly and gracefully. Of course, sometimes he can use his size to just plow through a play and make a "monster dunk," as he calls it.

Players must also be able to get along with teammates and communicate with them on the court. They must understand the strategy of the game and know how to create opportunities to make shots. They must be able to defend their basket and get the ball

Shaq may be big, but he's also fast.

into the other team's. And they need to be able to concentrate in order to shoot and score.

Shaq shows off one of the "monster dunks" that have made him famous.

Every player, even one as talented as Shaq, must practice, practice, practice. In all the excitement of Shaq's first season in the NBA, many people seemed to forget that he was still a rookie. Luckily, Shaq did not. He kept a cool head. He knew he still had a lot to learn and was the first to say so.

Shaq went to training sessions and practices. He showed up on time, ready to play hard and improve his game. Coaches and other players respected Shaq for his eagerness to learn. But even though everyone around was saying how great Shaq was, he still knew he could get better. He didn't feel that he was too good or too special to practice like all the other players. He wanted to work hard.

Pete Newell runs a training camp for NBA players. Shaq had signed up for his camp before joining the Orlando Magic. But once Shaq had signed a contract, Newell didn't expect the rookie to show up. Many players in Shaq's position would skip basketball camp. Once they have signed with an NBA team they feel they no longer need the practice they can get at camp. Some players worry about getting hurt before the beginning of the season. Some just think they are too good for camp. But not Shaq.

"He came here voluntarily," Coach Newell remembered. "I thought that was amazing. It really said something about the kid. You know, you can get hurt. It's no walk in the park."

Newell was also impressed with Shaq's attitude. "He's got the discipline and respect that are going to enable him to be as good as he'd like to be," Newell said. "He's an impressive guy."

Shaq's teammates and coaches liked him

because he didn't act as if he were the greatest player in the league, even if that's what many people were predicting.

Magic Johnson, former star of the Los Angeles Lakers, has said of Shaq, "He's got it all." Magic, who now does sports commentary, is not just talking about Shaquille O'Neal's skills as an athlete. On top of everything else, Shaq is a really great guy with a terrific smile, a concern for other people, and a goofy sense of humor.

Shaq's friends say that one of the best things about him is his "maxi-goofability!" Like the times he's dropped to the floor during a game to do a break-dance spin. Or when he's joined friends in rapping for a video cam. Or when he jokes with sportscasters and reporters, just to get a reaction out of them. Or when he gets a gang of his friends and family together and heads for Disney World to "have some fun, meet Mickey."

In his first year in the NBA, Shaq amazed many people. He was funny and charming. He played an impressive game but still worked hard to improve. He earned a huge amount of money. He had some moments that weren't perfect, but overall he made a good impression.

Some people said that after Shaq, basketball would never be the same.

3

Growing Up

Shaquille Rashaun O'Neal was born on March 6, 1972, in Newark, New Jersey. Shaquille Rashaun is an Islamic name that means "little warrior." When asked why she chose the name for her son, Lucille O'Neal, Shaq's mother, answered, "I wanted my children to have unique names. To me, having a name that means something makes you special."

At the time of his birth, Shaquille's parents were not yet married. Shaquille was given his mother's last name, and later decided to keep it as a way of showing his respect and love for her.

His father, Philip Harrison, was in the army and was stationed out of the country when Shaquille was born. When he returned home to the United States, he and Lucille began their life together. They lived in Newark, New Jersey. Soon they had other children.

Newark is a tough, poor city. The Harrisons worked hard to make ends meet. It wasn't always easy keeping food on the table, but they managed. It wasn't an easy place to grow up in, either. There were a lot of temptations that could get a kid into trouble.

"I was a little devious juvenile delinquent," Shaq has said. "Instead of being a leader, I was a follower. I would follow the so-called gangs." Although Shaq was punished when he misbehaved, he says it took a while for him to calm down. But eventually, he did.

The family moved a lot, as most military families do. Shaquille's father would be transferred to a different army base, and the whole family would have to pack up, move, and set down roots in a new place. By now, the whole family consisted of Shaq, his parents, two sisters, and three brothers.

Moving was interesting, but it was also hard on everyone. Shaq often wanted to go back to Newark to stay with his grandmother instead of moving around the world with his family. But his parents wanted the whole family to remain together. Shaq was—and still is—a good big brother to the whole bunch.

"The worst part," Shaq remembers, "was

traveling. Meeting people, getting tight with them—and then having to leave. Sometimes you come into a new place and they'll test you. I always got teased."

Shaquille was teased by the kids in new places because he had an unusual name. He was teased because he was the new kid. He was teased because he was so much bigger than the other kids his age. Shaq had grown to be so big, so quickly, that he was embarrassed about his size.

"My parents told me to be proud," Shaq says. "But I wasn't. I wanted to be normal." Like most kids his age, Shaq just wanted to fit in and be like everyone else. But he couldn't hide the fact that he was different. Even when he walked all slouched over, Shaquille still towered over everyone. He was clumsy and constantly tripped over his own two feet. Kids called him names like

*Although Shaq didn't always enjoy being so big, he has
learned how to put his size to good use!*

"Sasquatch"—Bigfoot. That made him mad.

Kids made jokes about him. They said
he had flunked and was bigger than them

because he ought to be in a higher grade in school. It wasn't true, of course, but it still hurt.

When Shaquille was in junior high, his family moved to a town called Fulda, in what was then West Germany. His father had been transferred to an army base there. It was the second time the family would live in West Germany, but it was not an easy move.

Some Germans were not happy about having an American military base in their country. They wanted the Americans to go away. There were demonstrations by the Germans. Once the Germans painted all the vehicles on the base bright blue as a protest.

But Shaq tried not to let this bother him. During this time, he was struggling with schoolwork and dreaming about what he really wanted to spend his time doing, like any other twelve-year-old boy.

As a young kid, Shaquille didn't think about growing up to be a basketball player. He wasn't especially interested in sports. His dream was to become a break dancer. The movie *Fame*—about students at the High School for the Performing Arts in New York City—made Shaq want to be a dancer. It seemed like a fun and exciting thing to be.

He imagined himself one day becoming a star. It was also a good way to get over being so clumsy. After years of practicing dancing and footwork in basketball, Shaq now says, "I'm mobile and *feet*-ile. I don't know what 'feet-ile' means, but I like the way it sounds."

Shaquille practiced break dancing until he could do perfect headspins like all the best break dancers. He could make his body practically slither along with the music. His natural strength and agility made him a very good dancer. And he had a lot of fun doing it.

But Shaq continued to grow. He grew, and grew, and grew. He had always been big for his age, but suddenly he was huge. By the time he was fourteen years old, he was six feet eight inches tall!

He was too big to spin on his head. And his body was too big and wide to move with the same loose flowing motions.

It was a terrible disappointment to him, but Shaq realized he was not going to grow up to be a dancer. He wasn't sure what he wanted now that he'd given up that dream. But soon he would find his way to basket-ball.

4

Basketball Beginnings

While Shaq and his family were living in Fulda, a man named Dale Brown was running a basketball clinic in Europe. Brown, the coach for the Louisiana State University (LSU) basketball team, was traveling around looking for new players to recruit for his team back in the United States.

One day Shaquille went to the basketball clinic to play. He hadn't been playing long,

As a professional basketball player, Shaq sometimes
faces opponents who are almost as big as he is,
like Patrick Ewing.

but he was beginning to like the game. He was also getting pretty good at it. Dale Brown saw Shaq and thought he was a young soldier. He was surprised to find out that Shaq was a soldier's son, barely a teenager! Remember, Shaq was already over six feet tall.

Coach Brown realized that Shaquille O'Neal could be an exceptional basketball player someday. He asked to meet the boy's father, and the two men talked about Shaq's possible future in basketball.

Brown encouraged Shaquille to work hard on improving his game. He looked forward to seeing how Shaq's talent would develop. Soon after their meeting, Brown continued his travels around Europe and returned to Louisiana.

Shaquille kept playing basketball. He was having fun with the game. He was getting better at it every day. He became less clumsy too. Playing basketball gave him a reason to feel good about being so big. That was a welcome change.

It took Shaq a bit longer to really feel proud of himself. But he was starting to feel comfortable with his size. He had stopped slouching. He was happy to be himself, big as he was.

"It took a while to gain friends because people thought I was mean," Shaq remembers. "I had a bad temper." When the teasing he got from other kids upset him, Shaq often got into fights.

Shaq has said, "My father stayed on me. Being a drill sergeant, he had to discipline his troops. Then he'd come home and discipline me." Shaq's parents were strict. They would not stand idly by watching their son misbehave. But they also loved their son and made sure he knew that.

Eventually Shaq realized that fighting wasn't solving any of his problems. So one day he began to just walk away from confrontations with troublemakers.

It took lots of practice for Shaq to become the amazing basketball player that he is today.

Shaquille's mother has said that watching Saturday morning cartoons also helped Shaq decide he was finished being a troublemaker and following a crowd. Superheroes like the Incredible Hulk, Spiderman, and others inspired him to grow up to be a leader. He wanted to be a good guy. He was also beginning to find a direction for some of his energy and a way to use his size. He began to work harder in school.

"When I was fifteen, I was big, and I realized I was pretty good at basketball," Shaq has said. "So that's what I decided to do." He was ready to take charge of himself.

"At about sixteen, I said, I'm going to be a leader. I'm going to do what I want to do, but I want to do the right thing."

It became easier to make friends when he didn't have a reputation for being a big, mean guy. Shaq decided to be funny instead of mean.

"My parents used to get notes all the time from my teachers," says Shaquille. "The notes would say 'Shaq is trying to be the class clown again.'" Still, this kind of trouble was better than hanging out with gangs and fighting.

About this time Sergeant Harrison, Shaq's father, got orders to move again to a new military base. Shaq and his family would be living in San Antonio, Texas.

5

High School

It was a big change to go from West Germany to Texas, but it was a good time to move. Shaq was about to start high school. And he was looking forward to playing basketball in America. Shaq soon became a local star.

Very quickly, everyone learned about the amazing basketball player at Robert Cole Senior High School in San Antonio. He was an all-American. That means he was one of the very best high school basketball players in the whole country.

But it wasn't easy for Shaq. He was working very hard at basketball. "I couldn't dunk a ball until the end of my junior year in high school," Shaq remembers. "I didn't give up. I just kept practicing every day. When everybody was going to parties and stuff like that, I was outside working on my coordination and trying to dunk."

In the meantime, Dale Brown was still coaching at LSU. Brown had not forgotten about Shaquille O'Neal. He kept up with Shaquille's game. He was not surprised by Shaq's success. Nor was he surprised that many other coaches were beginning to notice Shaq as well.

During his junior year at Cole, Shaq learned an important lesson. It was a lesson that would be useful to him years later when he would find himself in the spotlight as a rookie in the NBA.

Shaq's team had played thirty-five games

*Shaq hangs from the rim during his days as a
player for the LSU Tigers.*

without losing once during the season. They were now getting ready to play one of the final games for the state championship. It was against a team that everyone thought they would beat.

"There was a newspaper article that said that O'Neal and Cole should win state," Shaq recalls. "The guy was saying how I should come out and score fifty points and get sixty rebounds." Shaq believed the article. He decided to stay out late the night before the game, goofing around. He and his teammates were sure they would win without even trying. But the other team had a different idea.

"They just came out shooting," says Shaq. "They were killing us. They had us 21-2 in the first quarter and I had four fouls in the first two minutes." In high school basketball, after a player gets five fouls he is removed from the game. It seemed likely that Shaq would foul out long before the end of the game. Without Shaquille, Cole was sure to lose.

But somehow, Shaq managed to stay in the game. At the end of the fourth quarter, with only fifteen seconds left to play, and his team down by one point, Shaq was fouled. He had the chance for two free throws. This was his chance to turn things around and win the game. Shaq stepped to the line and took his first shot...and missed. He took his second shot...and missed again. Shaq's team lost!

After that game, Shaq decided not to believe everything he read about himself. He decided to take his opponents a little more seriously. And he decided to remember that he could be beaten anytime—so it was always important to play his best game.

When Shaq was a senior in high school, he played in an all-star game that was televised across the country. It was the first time that he was on national TV. It was the first time that people outside Texas got a chance to see what an incredible ballplayer Shaq was becoming.

In that game Shaq made an amazing play. It was an example of how he can do more than most centers, more than just get rebounds and put the ball up to score.

The play went like this: Shaq blocked a shot on defense, then grabbed the loose ball and dribbled the length of the court. He seemed to fly down the court. No one could stop him. Finally he leaped toward the basket and dunked the ball!

Even for a professional ballplayer that would have been an impressive play. For a high school kid, it was amazing. Many people watching the game thought that if he kept playing basketball that well, Shaquille O'Neal would be headed for the NBA.

Shaquille closed out his high school career by leading his team to a 68-1 record. During his senior year, his team didn't lose a single game. They also won the Class AAA state championship. *Parade* magazine named Shaquille O'Neal an all-American after he averaged 32.1 points, 22 rebounds, and 8 blocked shots per game during his senior year. He was named MVP of both the McDonald's All-Star Classic and the Dapper Dan Classic. That was an impressive record.

Dale Brown never lost touch with Shaq. As soon as he could, Coach Brown recruited Shaq for his team. Brown was expecting O'Neal to be a superstar. He wanted Shaquille to be on *his* team, not playing against it.

Shaq's parents let him make his own decision about which college to attend. LSU wasn't the only school that wanted him on their team. But Shaq liked Dale Brown, and LSU did have a strong team. It looked like a

Shaq and Rony Seikaly of the Miami Heat fight for position for a rebound.

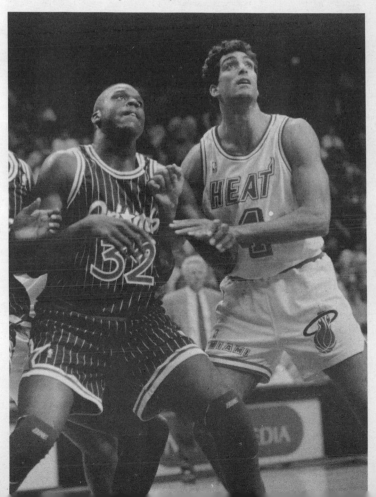

Shaquille O'Neal pulls up for a jump shot.

good place to learn to play a better game of basketball.

Shaq now had his eye on playing professionally. He felt that Dale Brown could help him reach that goal. When Shaq finally made his choice, his parents were happy for him. "Go out there and take what we taught you, and what you learned in life, and apply it. Do what you have to do," said his father.

So Shaquille left San Antonio to attend college in Louisiana. He was planning to study business. And to play basketball, of course.

6

College

In college Shaq studied hard. He was taking courses in business. He was also becoming a better basketball player.

In his second year of college, Shaquille broke his leg and couldn't play basketball for part of the season. Despite this he had a very good year. He was named Player of the Year by *Sports Illustrated* and several major news organizations. Scouts for the NBA, who were looking for new players, were watching Shaq very closely.

Shaq shows off his stuff at LSU.

But even with all this attention, Shaquille was still the same good-natured, goofy kid he had always been. He liked loud music, especially rap. He still liked to break dance. And he enjoyed doing crazy stuff, like most teenagers.

One summer he had a construction job at LSU. While he was working on the roof of a house, he decided it would be fun to jump off. And so he did. He startled the people living inside the house. But luckily he didn't hurt himself. It was only a one-story house.

Shaquille's parents had always said that they wanted him to finish college. They knew he was impatient to start his career, but they also felt it was important for him to have a college degree. They knew he wouldn't be able to play basketball forever. They wanted him to have an education so that he would be ready to deal with life after basketball.

After his second year at LSU, Shaq told his father that he wanted to leave. Shaq knew that he could play for the NBA and make a lot of money. He wanted to help out his family. But Shaq's father told him to stay in school. He didn't want Shaq to quit early just to make the family's finances easier to handle.

So Shaquille agreed to stay in school. Dale Brown knew that Shaquille was headed for the NBA. To help him get ready, Brown arranged for some of the best players in the NBA to come practice with Shaq. Kareem Abdul-Jabbar was one of the players who came to help him improve his game.

But even though Shaq's game was improving, things were getting worse. In his third year at LSU, Shaq started having a bad time with his team, the Tigers. He was beginning to find it frustrating to play college basketball.

Because Shaq was so big and so hard to beat, other teams were starting to gang up on

*Frustration shows on Shaq's face as
things start to get tough.*

him. The opposing team's strategy would not
be to play a good game and win by skill and
strength. Their strategy would simply be to
get Shaq out of the game.

They'd foul him as much as they could. They double-teamed—and triple-teamed—him. That's when two—or three—players guard a single player on the opposite team to keep him from scoring or getting the ball. It means other players are left unguarded. But against a player as powerful as Shaq, keeping him out of the game does more to help the other team's chances than guarding every player.

Yet even double-teaming wasn't enough to keep Shaq from scoring. Some teams would actually put as many as five men—a whole team!—on Shaq. It was impossible for him to play a decent game under such circumstances.

The vice president of an NBA team saw Shaq play against the University of Arkansas during his junior year at LSU. "They had five guys guarding O'Neal the whole time," he remembers. "I knew right then he wouldn't stay in college."

The games started getting much rougher. There were a lot of fights. Shaq was not having much fun anymore. Opposing teams would harass him and try to make him mad so that he'd start a fight or foul out of the game. Sometimes he spent most of his time on the bench. That began to happen more and more often.

When the Tigers made it to the Southeastern Conference tournament, things got really bad. Shaquille had tried to be patient throughout the difficult season. But during the tournament he lost his temper. He started a nasty fight that turned into a bench-clearing brawl. The game was suspended for twenty-five minutes. Players from both teams were ejected.

The next day, Shaq was suspended from

playing in the upcoming Southeastern Conference championship game. That was the last straw.

Shaq decided it would be best to leave school. He had had a satisfying career. He won many awards, including the Adolph Rupp Trophy for outstanding collegiate bas-

Shaq holds his opponent in a headlock during a brawl during the Southeastern Conference tournament.

Shaquille was awarded the Adolph Rupp Trophy for Outstanding Collegiate Basketball Player. At left is Randy Ayers of Ohio State, who received the coach of the year honor for 1990–91.

ketball player for the 1990-91 season and the James J. Corbett Memorial Award, given to the outstanding college athlete in Louisiana, for 1991. Shaquille O'Neal also received a National Achievement Award, presented to him at the White House, where he got to meet President George Bush.

During his junior—and final—year playing college basketball, Shaq averaged 5.2 blocks per game and was ranked number one in the country. He finished his career as the Southeastern Conference's leading shot

Shaq proudly displays the James J. Corbett Memorial Award, which he won in 1991. The award is given to the outstanding collegiate athlete in Louisiana.

Shaq meets President George Bush after being given a National Achievement Award.

blocker. He had blocked 412 shots in three years. He was second in the country in rebounding. His college statistics were impressive. He averaged 21.6 points, 13.5

rebounds, 4.6 blocks, and sixty-one percent shooting from the field.

But it was obvious that Shaq wasn't going to get anything more out of college basketball. He might spend his senior year sitting on the bench after fouling out of a game. Or

Shaq enjoyed an impressive career at LSU.

worse, he might get hurt trying to break through the unfair defenses he was up against, or in a fight.

He decided it was time to become a professional basketball player. His parents finally agreed. They could see that Shaq was unhappy playing basketball in college. He was ready to move on to a different, and, he hoped, more fulfilling, game.

7

The Magic

When Shaquille O'Neal decided to leave LSU, he let the people in charge of the NBA know that he was available for the draft. He made this announcement on April 3, 1992. He had to claim he was a "hardship case" in order to be considered.

Shaq stated that he and his family needed the income he would get as a professional basketball player. By showing that he was likely to be picked by an NBA team, he would be eligible for the 1992 draft.

In explaining his decision, Shaq also said that illegal physical action by his college opponents was the reason that college basketball was "no fun anymore."

The draft is one way that professional teams choose new players. There are twenty-seven teams in the National Basketball Association. The sixteen best teams play against one another in the play-offs at the end of the season. Each time a team loses a series, it is eliminated from the play-offs. Finally only the two best teams are left. The winning team is the NBA champion.

The eleven teams that don't make it into the play-offs are eligible to be part of a lottery that gives them the first picks of the new players coming into the league.

The Magic were the second worst team in 1991–92 and expected to get a good lottery pick. As an expansion team (one of the four teams recently added to the league) they still needed strong players to compete. They especially needed a strong center—someone like Shaquille O'Neal. Shaq was considered a number one draft pick. That meant he was one of the very best of the new players that teams could select.

Orlando was hoping to get a pick in the top four. They were thrilled when they got the number one pick! "I went blank," said Pat Williams, the man who manages the Orlando Magic. Williams is usually known for being very witty. He was so amazed that the Magic had won the first pick, he couldn't think of anything to say. Of course, the Magic would pick Shaquille O'Neal.

The lottery was televised. Within a minute of the announcement that Orlando had the number one pick, fans began calling to order season tickets!

Shaquille agreed to join the team. He was given a contract to play for the Magic for the next seven years. The team would pay him almost $40 million over those years. That was the biggest contract a rookie player had ever gotten!

Many people wondered if Shaquille O'Neal could possibly be good enough to justify the huge amount of money he was going to be paid. The Magic had to carefully arrange the salaries and contracts of their other players to make it possible to keep the deal they had agreed to.

But his future teammates and coach all believed he was worth it. "He's just an awesome physical presence," Magic point guard Scott Skiles said. "Any guard would love to play with someone like him."

"They don't come like that every day," said teammate Nick Anderson. "And you've

Number one draft pick Shaquille O'Neal joins the Orlando Magic.

got to take advantage of the opportunity when it's there." Soon most other people were agreeing.

Orlando is not only the hometown of the Magic. It is also where Disney World is located. On June 28, Shaq arrived in Orlando to sign his contract with the Magic. He got off the plane wearing Mickey Mouse ears.

Pat Williams gave him a tour of the city. They passed a huge billboard that said "Wel-

Shaq hugs NBA commissioner David Stern after the 1992 draft.

come, Shaq." Everyone in Orlando was thrilled that Shaq was coming to be a member of the Magic and a part of their city.

"This kid is going to light up the place like no one ever has before," Williams said to a crowd of Orlando businessmen.

The day after he signed his contract with the Magic, Shaq and his friends wanted to celebrate. In his contract it says that Shaq is not allowed to go sky-diving or ride a motorcycle. That is because he could get hurt doing such dangerous activities. And that would be bad for the team.

So, to have a good time, Shaquille and his buddies went to a water park. Then, instead of using a raft, Shaq let his friends climb on top of him and they went down the water slide together!

It soon became clear that Shaq had made the right decision by leaving college. By the middle of the season, Shaq had been named NBA Rookie of the Week, and Rookie of the Month, many times over. He had also cemented a place for himself at the center of his team.

Soon Shaq and forwards Dennis Scott and Nick Anderson became known as the Knuckleheads. When they are introduced before a game they run out on the court holding their fists, knuckles out, up to their foreheads. It's a funny name that started when rookie guard Litteral Green and Shaq were in college. They played against each other as captains of their respective teams.

"Before the game started, the ref would tell Shaq and me, 'All right, keep it clean, you knuckleheads,'" explains Litteral.

"The Knuckleheads—it's our fraternity," says Shaq. "It keeps us loose, keeps us together." Scott Skiles and Jeff Turner, the

Shaquille drives to the basket to score two points over the Phoenix Suns.

veterans in the Magic's starting lineup, are not Knuckleheads.

Shaq, Dennis, and Nick are fans of rap music. Sometimes they even rap together after practice. Skiles and Turner aren't rap fans. But even they get into the goofiness sometimes. One night before a game a funny picture was being passed around the locker room. It showed all five guys with huge afros drawn on so they looked like the Jackson Five. The caption read: "The Shaq-son Five."

It's good for a team to laugh together when they're off the court. It helps keep them in close communication when they are on the court. Shaq seems to have brought a lot of good feeling to the whole team. Everyone is infected with his good spirits.

Shaq was having a good time as a rookie on the Magic. He was making good friends. He was happy. He wasn't going to let all the pressure of measuring up to everyone's expectations get to him.

When reporters asked him how he would deal with the high expectations, Shaq answered, "One, I've got to have fun. Two, I can't worry. And three, I've got to play for me and nobody else."

8

Ultra-Fame

Almost overnight Shaquille O'Neal became famous. He was the number one pick in the 1992 lottery. He was the highest-paid rookie in the NBA. He was also the number one player that advertisers wanted to sign. And very early in his first NBA season, he was called the sport's first "ultra-star."

When Shaq was asked what he thought about all the attention he was getting, he said, "Some guys who are real good don't get the media attention. If a top media official says Shaq is a world champion, then people read that and say I'm a world champion. If someone says I'm a flop, as long as my family still loves me, I'm going to be all right."

Many companies try to get famous people to endorse the things they make. To endorse something is to say you like it, or use it. Advertisers think that if famous people say they like something, other people will want to buy it.

Famous athletes often endorse things like sneakers and sports equipment. It was not unusual for companies to want Shaq's endorsement. What was unusual was how quickly and carefully Shaq, his business manager, agent, and family created an endorsement empire. They chose the products that Shaq would lend his name to very carefully. They were also cautious about how Shaq was presented in commercials.

"I'm not going to make myself a super-hero that people can't touch," says Shaq. "The commercials are going to show both sides of me, including what I like to do off the court, like listen to rap music."

Before the end of his first NBA season, Shaq had signed contracts to endorse Reebok athletic shoes, Pepsi-Cola, Spalding sports equipment, and Kenner action figures. It seemed as though everyone wanted a little piece of Shaq.

He also developed his own logo. A logo is a piece of artwork, like a picture, that becomes a symbol for the company or person it represents. Shaq's logo is a symbol of a big guy dunking a basketball.

The logo is a simple idea, but a smart one. No one else had ever created a logo for an individual before. Then again, no one else had ever become such a huge business for just being himself before.

Shaq's logo has appeared on hats and T-shirts, sneakers and basketballs and more. The logo is just one of the good ideas that Shaq and his friends and family had when mapping out his business, One Al. The company is named to honor Shaq's mother. It uses the same letters as her name, O'Neal, but set up differently.

Shaq's mother, father, and a sister are all involved in the family business. His best friend from college is also a part of the business. They had all been looking forward to the day when Shaq would become a professional basketball player. And though no one could predict what a smashing success Shaq would be, they had some ideas ready when it happened.

Shaq became so popular so fast that products with his logo seemed to just disappear from stores. Manufacturers couldn't make hats and T-shirts fast enough to keep up with the demands of fans. In the Orlando Magic store, the shelves were emptied of anything bearing Shaq's logo almost as soon as they had been stocked.

And every time someone buys anything with Shaq's logo on it—for example, a T-shirt, a pair of socks, or a key chain—Shaq gets a royalty. A royalty is a small portion of the money from a sale that is paid to the person who owns the rights to that item. Shaq-mania has helped to sell a lot of merchandise. Add up all those little royalty payments and Shaq is making many thousands of dollars.

But Shaq isn't the only one benefiting from his fame. The Orlando Magic's stadium suddenly had every seat full during his first season. It was the first time in the team's four-year history that this had happened. Everyone wanted to see Shaq in action.

Many athletes have made fortunes endorsing products. Shaq's fortune may be as much as $50 million a year, just from endorsements. That doesn't include his salary from the Magic.

It might have been easy for people to take advantage of Shaquille O'Neal. Many athletes have been hurt by people who tried to use their fame to get rich.

Luckily, Shaq is surrounded by good business partners, family, and friends. He gets advice from all of them. He thinks carefully about his business deals and plans wisely. Although he is young, Shaq is smart. That is very important.

One of the most amazing things about Shaq is that he has not been changed by his sudden fame and fortune. Everyone who knows him says that Shaq is still the same fun-loving guy. He will still drop to the floor and do a break-dance spin, just to surprise people.

Shaq doesn't think having so much money matters. It doesn't change who a person is. But it does give him a chance to get a lot of fun stuff—like toys, video games, even cars and houses!

9
Off Court

During his rookie season with the Magic, Shaq bought a nice house in the fanciest neighborhood in Orlando. Even though it is very nice, Shaq's house cost less than $1 million. For somebody with as much money as he has, that is sort of surprising. Houses can be very expensive. Some very rich people spend many *millions* of dollars on their homes. But the house had everything that Shaq wanted. He is very happy with it.

Shaq's neighbors include doctors, businessmen, and real estate tycoons. It's a quiet neighborhood, unless Shaq's playing music. Then his house is the one with the walls shaking.

Shaq also had a house built nearby for his parents. After Shaq's father retires from the military his parents plan to move in. The family looks forward to being close again. During Shaq's first season in Orlando, they spoke on the phone at least once every day. But it was hard not being able to see their son often.

The neighborhood Shaq lives in is right in the middle of a huge golf course. Shaq doesn't like golf. But he did like the house, so that's where he decided to live.

One day, soon after Shaq had moved into his new house, Chicago Bulls star Michael Jordan, who was in town for an upcoming match between the Bulls and the Magic, was playing golf. He realized that he was near Shaq's house. Michael decided to visit Shaq. Unfortunately, Shaq was taking a nap and missed his famous visitor! He didn't hear the doorbell ring. Later, Jordan and Shaq met on the basketball court.

Shaq's house has a video arcade with his favorite games in it. Shaq loves to play video games. He especially likes to play video basketball. There's even a new Shaq video basketball game due to come out soon. Shaq also has a full-size Terminator II arcade game and a high-tech, 3-D, 360-degree interactive Virtual Reality game.

"I like my toys and I like my music," says Shaq.

Shaq also likes to watch movies. His favorite kinds of films are martial arts and gangster movies. But now that he's famous it is hard for him to go out to the theater.

In fact, one of the hardest things about his new life is that he can hardly go anywhere without being surrounded by crowds.

"When I want to be alone and think, I get in my truck and drive," says Shaq. It's one of the only times he can be alone. Shaq likes driving. He likes cars too. He bought a fancy Mercedes, but he didn't like it that much. He gave it to his mother.

His favorite car is a customized Ford Explorer. The front seat is farther back than normal to make room for his big body. It has a great stereo system. The windows are tinted and the wheels are chrome. The truck is burgundy colored and it has Shaq-Attack license plates.

One of Shaq's best friends is his teammate Dennis Scott. Dennis has been on the team since the 1990-91 season, so he's got some experience with talking to reporters and handling the pressure of being a pro ballplayer. Dennis watches out for Shaq.

Shaq thinks of Dennis as an older brother. It helps that Dennis, like Shaq, is young and wealthy. Shaq never has to worry that his friend is only interested in his fame or his

As well as being a great basketball player, Shaq has many other talents—like rapping!

money. Dennis has got enough of both already.

"I'm not going to let anyone mess up his head," Dennis says. "As long as I'm his friend, I'm going to make sure he's all right."

Most important, the two friends just like to hang out together. They talk about girls. They goof around and make silly faces. They keep each other company when the team travels.

They also sing rap songs. In fact, they both appeared with the rap group Fu Schnickens on the *Arsenio Hall* show.

In the locker room, their lockers are next to each other. During interviews Dennis will help Shaq out. Sometimes reporters just don't want to let Shaq go, he's so easy to talk to. But Dennis can always get Shaq out of the locker room and onto the court, despite the crowds of reporters always hoping for one

Shaquille O'Neal gives a trademark grin during a press conference at Orlando Magic Headquarters.

more joke or clever remark from Shaq.

Another friend of Shaq's is Sarafina Bel-tempo, owner of an Italian restaurant. She and her husband have a little place where

Shaq likes to eat before games. She knows just how to fix his favorite pre-game meal: spaghetti and meatballs, and two slices of cheese pizza, with a large orange soda.

"My biggest problem is knowing who to trust," Shaq has said. "Everybody wants something." But with his easygoing nature and common sense Shaq is on the right track. He is trying to enjoy his life and live it well.

10

Sharing the Wealth

By the end of 1993, Shaquille O'Neal already had more money than he could spend in a lifetime. He had fun buying things for himself, but he wasn't greedy. He bought things for friends and family as well. And he also tried to share his wealth with poor people.

"I think the world should be a better place," says Shaquille. "I get a sick feeling in my stomach when I see people living outside. You never know why they're there."

Shaq will often buy meals for homeless people whom he sees in his travels. He is not only generous. He truly cares about people, even though they might be strangers, even though they are poor and dirty and ragged.

Shaquille remembers what it was like in his own family when he was young. There wasn't much money. Sometimes finding the money to keep food on the table wasn't easy. "Hey, I've eaten on food stamps. When we lived in the projects in Newark, that's how we bought groceries."

Soon after the beginning of his first season in the NBA, reports appeared in newspapers of Shaq's generosity. Shaq was uncomfortable with all the media attention. He was not trying to get more articles in the newspaper when he decided to have a Thanksgiving dinner for 300 homeless people. He just wanted to do something for some of the homeless people near Orlando at Thanksgiving time. But soon the papers were all talking about "Shaq's-giving."

Shaq's dinner was a big success. Many of the people sharing in the meal didn't know who Shaq was. They didn't realize that he was a famous basketball star. But they did appreciate that he had arranged for them to have a good meal.

"Basketball is not everything in life," Shaq responded when asked if it bothered him that some of the guests at the meal he hosted didn't know him. It didn't matter to Shaq if they recognized him, he said, "as long as they can eat and they're happy."

Shaquille said grace before the meal—a turkey with all the trimmings! Then he stood behind a counter and helped by dishing out rice and peas. When everyone had been served, Shaq sat down and ate Thanksgiving dinner with them.

"It was the best Thanksgiving ever," he commented later.

When Christmas came around, Shaq wanted to find a way to help children who were too poor to get presents. So he went to the Center for Drug-Free Living. He was given a list from the Center, with the name and age of each needy child. Then Shaq thought carefully about what that child would enjoy most.

Shaq thought about each kid on the list. He tried to pick out the best presents he could think of for each child. By the time he was through, Shaq had bought several truck-loads of presents!

"It took me three trips. I brought all the stuff home and put it in my living room. We took a couple of days getting it all wrapped, then I delivered the toys."

Shaq comes flying down the court.

Shaq found this experience very rewarding. He is looking forward to many more years of choosing and wrapping up Christmas gifts for kids he doesn't even know.

In addition to helping out the poor, Shaq regularly visits sick children in hospitals. He talks to kids in schools about avoiding drugs and working hard to stay in school.

One weekday Shaq arrived at the Orlando city recreation complex to practice at around 11 A.M. The whole place was empty, except for one teenage boy sitting alone up in the bleachers. Shaq called to the boy and asked him what he was doing hanging around the complex when he ought to be in school. The boy said he wanted to watch the practice because he wanted to be a basketball player, like Shaq.

"You want to be like me?" Shaq asked. "You're not going to be like me if you don't

Shaq takes a breather during a game.

go to school and pass because it's no pass, no play." The boy soon headed for school.

Once a middle-school team from Massachusetts was playing basketball at the same university where Shaq was practicing before a Celtics game. The kids were impressed with how friendly he was.

"He did this kung fu thing—made a weird face," one boy said. "The guy is a real comedian. He's way more friendly than the other guys."

Being famous makes Shaq a role model to millions of kids. He takes that seriously. It isn't his job to fix the lives of all the kids who admire him, but Shaq wants to be the best person he can be, to set an example. He hopes that parents will help their own children, just as his did, to grow up wise and good.

Sometimes, when he's flying down the

court—with his arms and legs stiff, his eyes bulging, and his mouth open—Shaq can look pretty scary. But he's really a soft-hearted guy. And the frightening face he puts on during a game is often suddenly transformed by his smile.

11

What's Next?

Although the Magic didn't make it to the play-offs in 1993, Shaq had a great year. During the off-season, there was a lot to keep him busy. But most important of all was practicing.

Shaq worked hard to improve his game, especially when it involved shooting. He listened to the critics who said his offensive game needed work.

"I'll develop a reliable jump shot," he says. "But I don't expect it to be more than a diversion. I like contact. I want to get better every year, every month, every game. I'm paid too much money to sit back and get lazy."

During his rookie year Shaq also wrote and recorded his first rap songs. He had always had a good time rapping. Now he had started a career of it! Shaq had fun making the recording. A company called Jive Records produced the recording and released it at the end of 1993. Of course Shaq had to make music videos to promote his record too. And just for fun, he appeared in videos with some rapper friends of his.

After finishing his first music video, Shaq went to Los Angeles to work on a movie. It is called *Blue Chip*. It's an exciting action adventure, starring Nick Nolte, in which Shaq portrays a basketball player. Shaq kept this project top-secret. He wanted everyone

Shaq takes time out from the filming of Blue Chip *to do an interview.*

to be really surprised by his screen debut.

Shaq was having a great time doing all these different things. He was living out the dreams he had had as a kid. However, for now at least, basketball is his first love.

"I'm not an actor," says Shaq, "but I *am* an entertainer. I'm happy that fans like to see me play. I'm seven feet, 300 pounds. I dunk hard. I slide on the floor. I get rebounds. And hey, people like to see that. If I was a fan, I'd want to see Shaq play too."

The year was certainly a busy one for Shaquille O'Neal. He appeared on *Arsenio Hall*, and every other talk show host wanted to interview him. His face was on the cover of dozens of magazines. He was the starting center on the Eastern Conference All-Star team. He was also Rookie of the Year. There were more than twenty different trading cards of Shaq as a rookie!

Shaq ended his first season with impressive stats. He averaged 23.4 points and 13.9 rebounds. Not as good as Wilt Chamberlain's all-time rookie record of 37.6 points and 27.0 rebounds, but still in the range of some of the sport's best rookie players.

During his rookie year Shaq was always the first to arrive at practice. And he was the last to leave. On the plane to away games, he sat with Orlando Magic coach Matt Guokas and talked about the game. They discussed strategies Shaq could use while playing. They also talked about how Shaq could work to the best advantage of the other players on the Magic. Shaq is very, very important to the whole strategy of the team.

"Anytime Shaq goes out of the game," Coach Guokas has said, "we're just not the same team. We can get by for a few minutes, hold down the fort for short stretches, but he is so involved in what we do."

Having such a famous and celebrated teammate might have made some players jealous, but Shaq's teammates really like him.

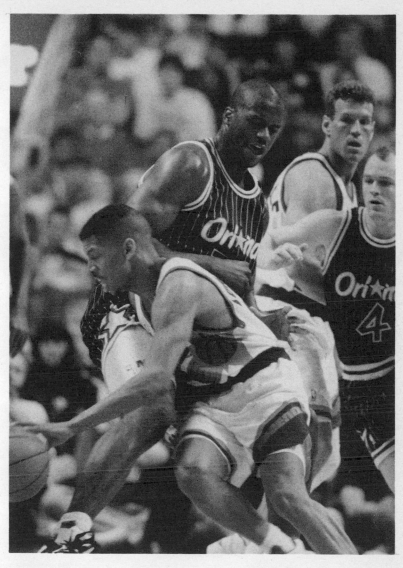

Shaq and teammate Scott Skiles attempt to block
Kevin Johnson of the Phoenix Suns.

They don't seemed bothered by his success. That probably has to do with Shaq's attitude more than anything else. Instead of acting like a superstar, Shaq is a real team player.

"I'm sure everybody wants me to carry this team on my back," Shaq has said. "But if we don't play together, none of that's going to be possible; I don't care who we have on the team."

Shaq also helps his teammates play a better game. Dennis Scott gets more chances to shoot because teams double-cover Shaq, leaving him alone. Nick Anderson has more room to slash to the basket because the other team's defense has to get around Shaq before they can get to him.

His coach, teammates, friends, and family, not to mention the fans, all respect and love Shaq. Everyone will be watching to see how Shaq improves as a ballplayer and if he con-

A rare moment on the bench for Shaquille O'Neal.

tinues to show the world how talented he is in other areas as well. It's a sure thing that he will do both.

"He knows he is going to make mistakes, but he also knows he is building toward something that is going to take time," says Coach Guokas. "We want Shaq to be as sound a player as possible, and he knows that being as good as you can be doesn't come with shortcuts."

So what is next for Shaquille? His friend Dennis Scott says that most of all Shaq wants to win the NBA championship.

Another teammate, Scott Skiles, says this about Shaq: "He could go out, not get any better than he is, and still be one of the better players in the league. Or he could get a taste of what he can be and become so good that he can be the best player in the league, and lift a whole organization to a championship."

And who knows, maybe 1994 will be the year the Magic win it!

STEPHANIE ST. PIERRE is the author of over thirty books for children, including *Jim Henson, Creator of the Muppets™*, *The Story of the Star-Spangled Banner*, and *Everything You Need to Know When Your Parents Are Out of Work*. In addition to her nonfiction work, she has written fiction for children of all ages. Ms. St. Pierre lives with her husband and two children in Brooklyn, New York.

Bullseye Biographies